放翁乡韵

陆游咏越诗词选编

绍兴文化广电旅游局 编

西泠印社出版社

2025年是陆游(1125－1210)诞辰900周年，谨以此书作为献礼

The year 2025 marks the 900th anniversary of the birth of Lu You (1125–1210), and this book is presented as a gift to convey our respects.

目录

contents

诗

词

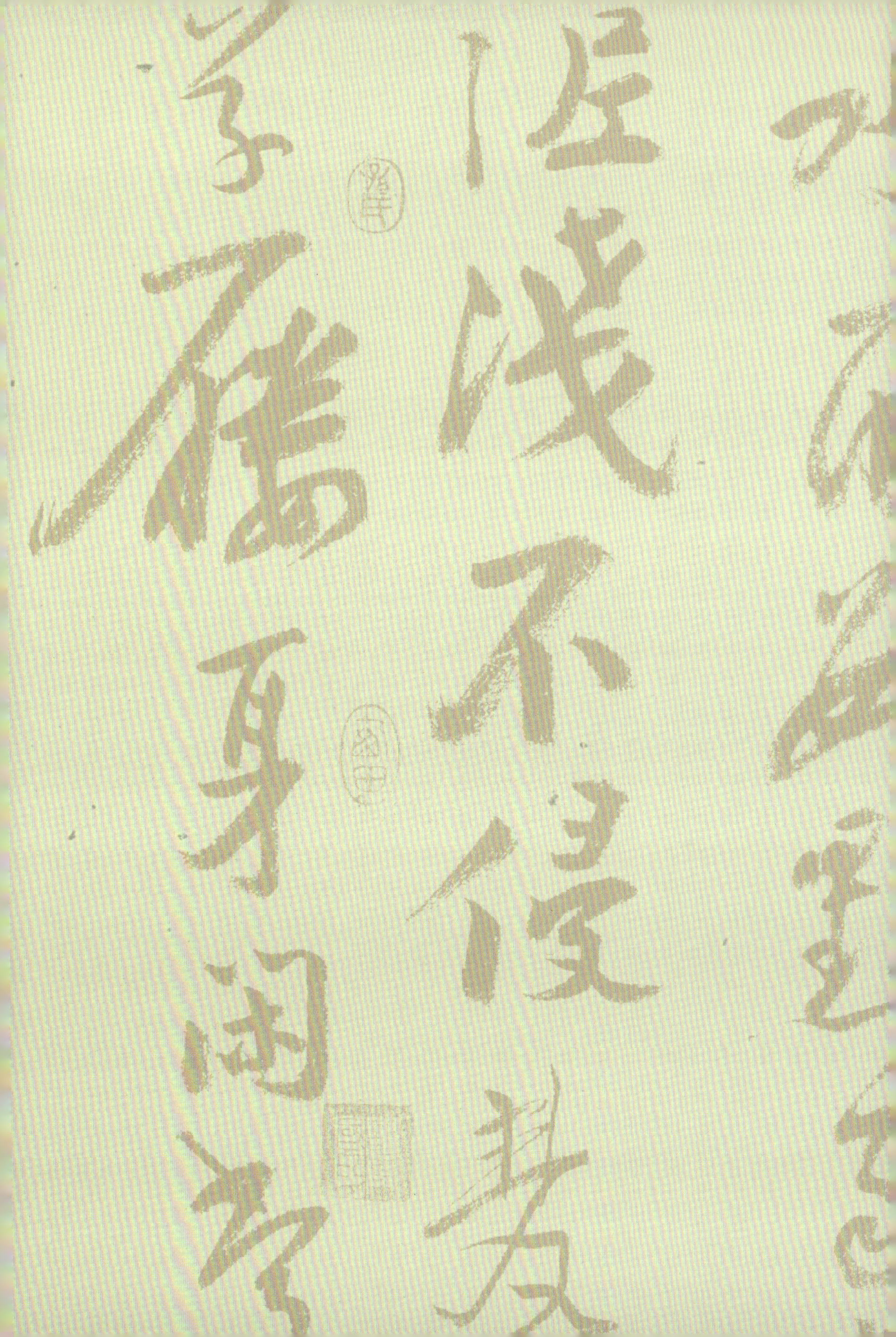

陆游

诗 

Poetry

舟中作

Composed on the Boat

沙路时晴雨，渔舟日往来。
村村皆画本，处处有诗材。
炊黍孤烟晚，呼牛一笛哀。
终身看不厌，岸帻兴悠哉！

沙路上时晴时雨，打鱼船每日往来。
村村美得皆可画，处处都有作诗材。
晚炊的孤烟升起，呼牛的笛声悲哀。
湖山终身看不厌，头束高巾乐开怀！

It is interinittent clear and rainy on sandy paths,
Fishing boats come and go every day.
Every village is pretty to be painted,
Everywhere is material for poetry.
From evening meal rises a solitary smoke,
The flute whistles for the cattle mournfully.
I never tire of seeing lakes and hills all my life,
Wearing a high scarf and enjoying the leisurely joy!

采莲曲

Lotus Picking Melody

采莲吴姝巧笑倩，小舟点破烟波面。
双头折得欲有赠，重重叶盖羞人见。
女伴相邀拾翠羽，归棹如飞那可许？
倾鬟障袖不应人，遥指石帆山下雨。

吴地的采莲姑娘笑得美，小船儿点破了烟波湖面。
折得个双头莲欲有所赠，却以莲叶遮盖羞被人见。
女伴相约拾些翠绿荷叶，归家小船飞快哪里容许？
以袖挡着脸低头不应人，远远指着石帆山在下雨。

The girls in Wu area picked lotus with charining smiles,

Breaking the surface of mist–covered waters with their small boats.

One picked a double–head lotus to offer as a gift,

Shy to be seen beneath the layers of leaves.

Girl companions agreed to pick up some jade green lotus leaves mutually,

But the returning boats were fast like flying, how could they be allowed to stop ?

Covering her face with sleeves and lowering her head,

She didn't answer but pointed to the rainy Shifan Mountain far away.

稽山行

Song of the Kuaiji Mountain

稽山何巍巍，浙江水汤汤。
千里亘大野，勾践之所荒。
春雨桑柘绿，秋风粳稻香。
村村作蟹椵，处处起鱼梁。
陂放万头鸭，园覆千畦姜。
舂碓声如雷，私债逾官仓。
禹庙争奉牲，兰亭共流觞。
空巷看竞渡，倒社观戏场。
项里杨梅熟，采摘日夜忙。
翠篮满山路，不数荔枝筐。
星驰入侯家，那惜黄金偿。
湘湖莼菜出，卖者环三乡。
何以共烹煮？鲈鱼三尺长。
芳鲜初上市，羊酪何足当？
镜湖蓄众水，自汉无旱蝗。
重楼与曲槛，潋滟浮湖光。
舟行以当车，小伞遮新妆。
浅坊小陌间，深夜理丝簧。
我老述此诗，妄继古乐章。
恨无季札听，大国风泱泱。

会稽山多么巍峨，钱江水浩浩荡荡。
大野绵延一千里，是勾践开垦之荒。
春雨时桑柘变绿，秋风中粳稻飘香。
村村设捕蟹之椵，处处建拦鱼之梁。
池塘内放万头鸭，菜园中种千畦姜。
舂米之碓声如雷，私家储粮超官仓。
禹庙里争供祭品，兰亭中曲水流觞。
万人空巷看船赛，春社散了观戏场。
项里村中杨梅熟，采摘之人日夜忙。
山路满是杨梅篮，更有无数荔枝筐。

星夜驰送侯王家，哪惜重金把鲜尝。
每当湘湖莼菜出，到处都是卖菜郎。
拿啥与之一起煮？可用鲈鱼三尺长。
芬芳鲜果初上市，羊酪何能敌其香？
镜湖蓄满众溪水，汉朝以来无旱蝗。
湖边高楼与曲栏，浮映浩瀚湖水上。
乘船可代乘车行，常以小伞遮新妆。
城中街坊与乡间，深夜有乐器奏响。
老了我写这首诗，敢望继写古乐章。
恨无知音季札听，大国风范深而广。

How towering is the Kuaiji Mountain!
The Qianjiang River is mightily flowing.
The great field stretches thousands of miles,
Which is the wasteland opened up by Gou Jian.
The mulberry trees turn green during the spring rain,
In autumn wind the fragrance of rice is wafting.
Each village sets up tools for crab catching,
Everywhere builds beams for fish blocking.
There are thousands of ducks in the pond,
And thousands of ginger are planted in the vegetable garden.
The hammer pounding rice sounds like thunder.
The official granary is exceeded by the private grain storage.
In the Yu Temple sacrifices are completed to enshrine.
People share the game of flowing water with cups in Lanting.
The whole town turns out to watch the boat racing.
People go to the theater after the Spring Sacrifice.
In Xiangli Village the spring waxberries are ripe,
Day and night people are busy picking.
The mountain road is full of waxberry baskets,
There are also lychee baskets beyond counting.

The fruits are rushed to wealthy families,
Rich men do not stint gold to taste a fresh thing.
Whenever the water shield appears in Xianghu Lake,
Everywhere vegetable sellers can be seen.
Is there anything that can be cooked with it ?
A three–foot–long bass is the suitable thing.
When sweet fruits first appear on the market,
How can goat cheese be as good as them in comparison ?
The Mirror Lake is filled with water from numerous streams,
Since the Han Dynasty no drought or locust there has been.
On the vast surface of the lake water,
Are high buildings with curved railing.
Taking a boat can replace taking a car,
Women often use umbrellas to cover their new makeup.
In the city and the countryside,
Late at night musical instruments are heard playing.
As I grow old, I write this poem,
Dare to continue the ancient music writing.
I hate no soulmate in music like Ji Zha comes to listen,
Deep and wide, the great country is bearing !

兰亭道上

On the Road to Lanting

湖上青山古会稽，
断云漠漠雨凄凄。
篮舆晚过偏门市，
满路春泥闻竹鸡。

湖上青山就是古会稽山，
天空碎云密布春雨凄凄。
我乘竹轿傍晚过偏门集，
满路春泥听得声声鸡啼。

The green mountain on the lake is the old Kuaiji Mountain,
The sky is covered with broken clouds and miserable rain.
I take a bamboo sedan to pass by the Pianmen Market at dusk,
On the road full of spring mud chickens are heard crying.

小雨泛镜湖

Boating on the Mirror Lake in Light Rain

吾州清绝冠三吴，
天写云山万幅图。
龙化庙梁飞白雨，
鹤收仙箭下青芜。
菱歌袅袅遥相答，
烟树昏昏淡欲无。
端办一船多贮酒，
敢辞送老向南湖？

我州山青水绿三吴称冠，
天然风景好似万幅画图。
龙化作庙梁如飞洒白雨，
鹤落下草地似仙箭收束。
菱歌不断传来遥相呼应，
烟树光线昏暗影淡如无。
我得置办一船多贮好酒，
度此余生怎能不去南湖？

Our prefecture is crowned in Three Wu with green mountains and clear rivers,
Its natural landscape looks like thousands of paintings.
The dragon turns into a temple beam like white rain flying,
Like a fairy arrow packed up, the crane falls on the grasses.
Echoing each other at a distance, songs of picking water–caltrop keep coming,
The misty trees are dimly lit and the shadows are as faint as nothing.
I have to prepare a boat with a lot of good wine,
How can I not go to the South Lake to spend the rest of my life ?

镜湖女

Mirror Lake Girls

湖中居人事舟楫，家家以舟作生业。
女儿妆面花样红，小伞翻翻弄荷叶。
日暮归来月色新，菱歌缥缈泛烟津。
到家更约西邻女，明日湖桥看赛神。

湖中有人操弄舟和桨，家家以行船作为生计。

女儿们脸孔花一样红，翻弄着小伞似的荷叶。

傍晚归来已新月一轮，菱歌袅袅荡漾在烟津。

回到家里约邻居女伴，明日到湖桥上看赛神。

People in the lake are boating and paddling,

Every family makes a living by sailing.

The girls' faces are as red as flowers,

They flip through lotus leaves like umbrellas.

Coming back in the evening is a crescent moon already.

The endless songs of picking water-caltrop ripple on the misty ferry.

Coming home they invited their neighboring girlfriends

To go tomorrow to the Lake Bridge to see the god competition.

思故山

Missing My Native Mountains

千金不须买画图，
听我长歌歌镜湖。
湖山奇丽说不尽，
且复为子陈吾庐。
柳姑庙前鱼作市，
道士庄畔菱为租。
一弯画桥出林薄，
两岸红蓼连菰蒲。
陂南陂北鸦阵黑，
舍西舍东枫叶赤。
正当九月十月时，
放翁艇子无时出。

船头一束书，
船后一壶酒。
新钓紫鳜鱼，
旋洗白莲藕。
从渠贵人食万钱，
放翁痴腹常便便。
暮归稚子迎我笑，
遥指一抹西村烟。

不用花费千金去买画图，
请听我用长歌歌唱镜湖。
湖山的雄奇秀丽说不尽，
还要为你把我家说一说。
柳姑庙前卖鱼成了集市，
道士庄边可用菱来交租。
一弯画桥现出稀疏树林，
两岸的红蓼连着菰与蒲。
坡南坡北歇着阵阵黑鸦，
屋西屋东都长有红枫树。
每当九月里或是十月时，
放翁小船不定时地驶出。

船头放着一捆书，
船后备有一壶酒。
新钓到的紫鳜鱼，
刚洗过的白莲藕。
跟那些贵人一顿吃万钱，
放翁吃饱常是大腹便便。
晚上归来孩子迎着我笑，
远远指着一抹西村的烟。

You don' t have to spend a lot of money on a drawing,
A long song about the Mirror Lake I' ll for you sing.
The majesty and beauty of the lake and mountain are beyond description.
About my house I need to tell you something.
Selling fish in front of the Liugu Temple has become a market,
Beside the Taoist Villa to pay the rent you can use water–caltrop.
A curved painted bridge emerges from the sparse trees,
On both banks red polygonum and wild rice are connecting.
On the south and north slope rest bursts of black crows,
In the west and east of the house maple trees are reddening.
Whenever in September or October
Irregularly sails out, the small boat of Fangweng.
There is a bundle of books in the bow of the boat,
In the back of the boat there is a pot of wine.
Newly caught mandarin fish,
White lotus roots freshly washing.
Eat ten thousand yuan with those noble men,
When he is full, Fangweng often has a large belly.
When I came back at night, the child greeted me with a smile,
Pointing at a hint of smoke from the distant west village.

赛神曲

Offering Sacrifices to Thank Gods

击鼓坎坎，
吹笙呜呜。
绿袍槐简立老巫，
红衫绿裙舞小姑。
乌臼烛明蜡不如，
鲤鱼糁美出神厨。
老巫前致词，
小姑抱酒壶：
愿神来享常欢娱，
使我嘉谷收连车；
牛羊暮归塞门闾，
鸡鹜一母生百雏；
岁岁赐粟，
年年蠲租；
蒲鞭不施，
圜土空虚；
束草作官但形模，
刻木为吏无文书；
淳风复还羲皇初，
绳亦不结况其余。
神归人散醉相扶，
夜深歌舞官道隅。

击鼓咚咚，

吹笙呜呜。

槐树中间立着穿绿袍的老巫，

穿着红衣绿裙的小姑娘跳舞。

乌桕做的烛比白蜡还要明亮，

鲤鱼做的羹味道美出于神厨。

老巫走上前致词，

小姑娘抱着酒壶：

愿神时常高兴前来享受祭品，

使我们年年丰收粮食车连车；

傍晚时牛羊归来塞满了庭院，

一只母鸡或母鸭生下百只雏；

岁岁赐给我们粟米，

年年为我们减租赋；

没有蒲鞭抽打我们，

土牢空空没有人住；

用稻草扎一官员只做做样子，

用木头刻一笔吏却没有文书；

淳朴风气恢复到当初羲皇时，

也不结绳记事何况家有粮余。

祭神后喝醉的村人相扶散去，

夜深了官道上还有人在歌舞。

Dong–dong is the sound of drumming,
Wu–wu is the sheng blowing.
Among locust trees stood an old witch in a green robe.
Little girls in red clothes and green skirts were dancing.
A candle made of Chinese tallow is brighter than that made of white wax,
The delicious taste of carp soup comes from magic cooking.
The old witch stepped forward to deliver a speech,
The little girl was holding the wine pot.
May gods often be pleased to come and enjoy the sacrifices,
So that we can harvest grain every year.
In the evening cattle and sheep come back to fill the courtyard,
A hen or duck gives birth to hundreds of chicks.
Give us corn every year,
Give us rent relief every year.
Without a whip to whip us,
The dungeon is empty and on prisoner lives there.
Using straw to make an official is just a posture.
Carve a government clerk out of wood, who has no work of paper.
The simple atmosphere has returned to the time of Emperor Xi,
Our families have surplus food, we need not tie to remember.
After the worship, the drunken villagers helped each other disperse,
Late at night, on the official way, there are people still singing and dancing there.

初夏

Early Summer

剪韭腌齑粟作浆，
新炊麦饭满村香。
先生醉后骑黄犊，
北陌东阡看戏场。

又

槐柳成阴雨洗尘，
樱桃乳酪并尝新。
古来江左多佳句，
夏浅胜春最可人。

剪韭成末腌,小米熬粥汤,
新煮的麦饭满村里飘香。
先生我醉后骑着黄牛犊,
沿北路走东路去看戏场。

槐柳相聚成阴雨洗其尘,
樱桃配上乳酪一并尝新。
自古以来江南颇多佳句,
初夏胜过春天最为可人。

Cutting and marinating chives, boiling millets into porridge,
Newly cooked wheat rice are fragrant all over the village.
Riding a yellow calf while drunk, a scholar,
I, along the north or east road, go to the theatre.

The shade of locusts and willows is washed by rain,
Let's taste cherry together with cheese.
Jiangnan has had good lines since ancient times,
Early summer is more charming than spring.

督下麦雨中夜归

Returning in Wheat Rain from Duxia at Night

力作不知劳，归路忽已夜。
犬吠闯篱隙，灯光出门罅。
岂惟露沾衣？乃有泥没胯。
谁怜甫里翁，白首学耕稼。
未言得一饱，此段已可画。

努力耕作不知疲劳，归路忽然已经入夜。
犬吠闯出篱笆间隙，灯光射出门的缝隙。
难道只是露水沾衣？还有泥巴淹没到胯。
有谁可怜文弱老翁，头发白了还学耕稼。
虽说未能吃得一饱，这段生涯已可描画。

I was farming tirelessly,

The way home fell into the night suddenly.

The dog barked through the gap of the fence,

The light shone through the gap of the door.

Is it just dew on my clothes ?

Or is there mud covering the crotch.

Who pities a frail old man

Learning to farm when his hair whiten ?

Although I haven't had enough to eat,

This period of life can already be painted.

偶得双鲫

Double Crucians Obtained Occasionally

今朝溪女留鲜鲫，
洒扫茅檐旋置樽。
养老不须烦祝鲠，
从来楚俗惯鱼餐。

今天溪边有女孩留了条鲫鱼，
我洒扫了茅屋随即置备酒杯。
老来无须人提醒会被鱼鲠刺，
南方的习俗一向把鱼当饭吃。

Today, a girl by the stream left me a fresh crucian carp,
Having swept the cottage I prepared a cup of wine.
In old age,I don't need to be reminded that I might get a fish bone stuck in my throat,
The custom in the south has always been to eat fish as a meal.

梅花绝句

Quatrain of Plum Blossims

闻道梅花坼晓风，
雪堆遍满四山中。
何方可化身千亿，
一树梅前一放翁。

我听说梅花绽放于晨风，
大雪堆满了各处的山中。
有何方法变成千万个我，
每一梅前站有一个放翁。

Plum blossoms bloom in the morning breeze, I hear,
Snow is piling up the mountains here and there.
What method can make a million of me:
A Fangweng stands in front of a plum blossom tree.

溯溪

Stream Tracing

射的山前禹庙东，短篷三扇卧衰翁。
闲携清圣浊贤酒，重试朝南暮北风。
水落痕留红蓼节，雨来声满绿蒲丛。
冲烟莫作匆匆去，拟看溪丁下钓筒。

在射的山之前，禹王庙之东，三扇短篷的小船上卧着衰翁。
闲来带着圣贤喝的清酒浊酒，重新测试早晨南风傍晚北风。
水落下去在红蓼上留下痕迹，下起雨来声音响满绿色蒲丛。
莫要打算冲破雨烟匆匆离去，而要观看溪边人如何下钓筒。

East of the Yu Temple, before the Shedi Mountain,
On a small boat with three canopies lay an old man.
He leisurely brings clear or turbid liquor for saints,
Retests south wind in the morning and north wind in the evening.
The water falls, leaving traces on the red polygonum.
When it rains, the sound fills the cattail bushes green.
Don't plan to rush away through the misty rain,
But watch how people set up fishing tubes by the stream.

初夏怀故山

Missing the Hometown Mountain in Early Summer

镜湖四月正清和，
白塔红桥小艇过。
梅雨晴时插秧鼓，
蘋风生处采菱歌。
沉迷簿领吟哦少，
淹泊蛮荒感慨多。
谁谓吾庐六千里，
眼中历历见渔蓑。

镜湖四月里天气真正清和，
白塔旁红桥下有小艇驶过。
梅雨季天晴时响起插秧鼓，
蘋风生处人们唱起采菱歌。
沉迷于簿册吟诵诗词也少，
漂泊在荒野之地感慨良多。
谁说过我的家乡六千里阔，
清清楚楚看见的都是渔蓑。

In April, the weather of Mirror Lake is temperate and clear,

A small boat passes under the red bridge next to the white pagoda.

When sunny in the plum rain season, drums sound for rice transplanting,

Where the gentle breeze blows, people sing the song of water–caltrop picking.

When indulging in official books we recite rarely,

Wandering in the wildness makes us sigh with emotion.

Who said that my hometown is six thousand miles wide,

What I can clearly see were straw rain capes for fishing.

小飲梅花下作

小饮梅花下作

Written while Drinking under the Plum Blossom

脱巾莫叹发成丝，
六十年间万首诗。
排日醉过梅落后，
通宵吟到雪残时。
偶容后死宁非幸？
自乞归耕已恨迟。
青史满前闲即读，
几人为我作蓍龟？

脱下头巾莫叹发成银丝，
六十年间吟得万首小诗。
天天醉酒梅落后还未醒，
通宵苦吟直到雪残之时。
偶然多活难道不是幸运？
我恨自己要求归耕已迟。
眼前堆满史书闲即可读，
几人为我占卜做过预期？

With my scarf taken off, I don't sigh my hair is silvery,

I have composed thousands of poems in the sixty years.

I get drunk every day and haven't woken up till plum blossoms fall,

Until the snow was gone I spent the night reciting poetry.

Isn't it lucky for me to live a few more years occasionally ?

I hate myself for asking to return to farming late already.

With many historical books piled up before me, I can read them when free.

How many people have prophesied with tortoiseshell for me ?

村市醉归

Drunken Returning from Rural Market

明时乞得水云身，
白首扶衰又见春。
横木门幽谢来客，
独辕车小避行人。
湘湖水长莼丝滑，
兰渚泥融箭茁新。
处处酒垆皆可醉，
不辞微雨垫吾巾。

我从圣明时代获得闲云流水之身，
头发白了又能扶正衰体重见新春。
我用横木拴门保持幽静谢绝来客，
推的也是小小的独轮车避开行人。
湘湖水中已长出丝丝滑溜的莼菜，
冰雪消融的兰亭泥土里突发新笋。
各处的酒店都可以让人尽兴喝醉，
我也不怕在小雨中醉倒垫上披巾。

Good time makes me free like clouds floating and water flowing,

With white hair, I can restore the aging body and see the new spring.

To keep quiet, I lock the door with a crossbar to refuse visitors,

And push a small unicycle to avoid any passers.

In the water of Xianghu Lake there have grown slippery water shield.

New bamboo shoots burst from the snow and ice melted soil of Lanting.

Wineshops everywhere can make people enjoy themselves and get drunk,

With a shawl under my body, I do not refuse to get drunk in light rain.

闲意

Leisure

柴门虽设不曾开，为怕行人损绿苔。
妍日渐催春意动，好风时卷市声来。
学经妻问生疏字，尝酒儿斟潋滟杯。
安得小园宽半亩，黄梅绿李一时栽？

虽然设有柴门但未曾开，因为怕行人损毁了绿苔。
明媚阳光渐渐催动春意，好风时时把买卖声卷来。
学经的妻子问我生疏字，尝酒儿子斟了满满一杯。
小园如何才能再宽半亩，好将那黄梅绿李同时栽。

The wicket door has never been opened although there is,

For fear that people might trample on the green moss.

The bright sunshine stimulates the spring mood gradually,

Good wind always brings the sound of business.

My wife who studies the classics asks me about unfamiliar words,

My son, tasting wine, pours a full cup.

How can my small garden be widen by half mu,

So that yellow and green plums are planted simultaneously?

村邻会饮

Drinking Together with Village Neighbors

陆子白首安耕桑，
乐事遽数乌能详？
长罗家家雪作面，
画楫处处青分秧。
迎获船归潮入浦，
祈蚕会散月满廊。
有时邻曲苦招唤，
茅檐扫地罗壶觞。
堆盘珍脍似河鲤，
入鼎大脔胜胡羊。
披绵黄雀曲糁美，
斫雪紫蟹椒橙香。
老人饱食可无患，
摩挲酒瓮与饭囊。
儿孙扶侍递相送，
笑语无间歌声长。
人间哀乐不可常，
掠剩有鬼在汝傍。
常忧水旱虞螟蝗，
力行孝悌招丰穰。

陆子我头发白了安心农桑，
快乐事怎能一下子说端详？
家家用长箩把面筛得雪白，
处处画船载来待分的青秧。
载苇船乘着退潮归入河口，
祈蚕会散场月色撒满走廊。
有时村邻们苦苦把我召唤，
茅檐下扫清地面罗列酒觞。
满盘珍馐美味好像是河鲤，
放入鼎煨的大块肉胜胡羊。
羽丰黄雀酒糟来吃味很美，
雪白的紫蟹肉蘸橙椒更香。
老人吃饱了可保没有害处，
轻轻抚摩着酒瓮似的肚囊。
他们由儿孙扶持着送回家，
路上笑语不间断歌声远扬。
人间悲哀快乐不可能常在，
劫掠剩物必有鬼在你身旁。
常忧水旱灾也怕螟蝗虫害，
孝父母爱兄弟定丰收增粮。

I, Lu You, with white head, engages in farming and sericulture,
How can happy things be told in detail immediately ?
Each family uses a long sieve to sift the flour until snow white,
Everywhere painted boats carrying undivided seedlings are in sight.
On the ebb tide the boat carrying reeds returned to the estuary,
The praying for silkworm dispersed and the corridor was full of moonshine.
Sometimes the village neighbors summoned me earnestly,
Sweeping the floor of a hut and setting out cups of wine.
The delicacies piling on the plate looks like river carp,
Large pieces of meat simmered in cauldron are better than Hu sheep.

The yellow finch is delicious to eat with distiller's grains.

Snow–white purple crab meat dipped in orange pepper tastes much better.

When old men eat their fill, they will meet impunity.

He can gently touch his jar–like belly.

They are carried home by their children and grandchildren,

Laughing and singing all the way.

It is impossible for the world to be always sad or happy,

If your remains are plundered, you are surrounded by ghosts probably.

We often worry about flood and drought, and fear borers and locusts.

Honoring parents and loving brothers will reap a bumper harvest surely.

山村经行因施药

Applying Medicine when Passing Through a Mountain Village

闲行偶复到山村，
父老遮留共一尊。
曩日见公孙未晬，
如今已解牧鸡豚。

又

驴肩每带药囊行，
村巷欢欣夹道迎。
共说向来曾活我，
生儿多以陆为名。

闲来步行偶然又到小山村，
有老者将我挽留共饮一樽。
先前见君之孙尚未满周岁，
如今已懂得如何放牧鸡豚。

每次我在驴肩带上药袋行，
村巷中人们把我夹道欢迎。
都说以前是我救活了他们，
生了小孩大多以陆为其名。

I occasionally wandered to a small mountain village again,
An old man asked me to stay for a cup of wine.
Previously, I saw your grandson had not reached the age of one,
Now he knows how to graze pigs and chicken.

Every time I carry a medicine bag on the shoulder of a donkey,
People gave me a welcome by lining the village alley.
They all say I've always brought them to life,
Most of born children are named after Lu certainly.

村居

Rusticate

黍酒浓浮瓮，瓜菹绿映盘。

老便藜粥美，病喜粟浆酸。

纱帽新裁稳，绝袍旧制宽。

村居亦何好？聊用发诗端。

浓浓的高粱酒浮在瓮中,绿绿的腌黄瓜堆满一盘。

人老了粗粮粥也觉得美,生病了喜欢小米浆的酸。

新裁的纱帽戴起来很稳,旧尺寸的粗绸袍子太宽。

住在乡村究竟有何好处? 聊以启发诗思创作诗篇。

Thick sorghum liquor floats in the jar,

A plate is filled with green pickled cucumbers.

When people get old, coarse grain porridge is sweet,

When they are sick, they like sour boiled pulp of millet.

Stable to wear is the gauze hat cut newly,

The old size of the thick silk robe is too wide.

What are the benefits of living in the countryside ?

Inspiring poetic thoughts to create poetry.

东篱

East Fence

东篱深僻懒衣裳，书卷纵横杂药囊。
无吏征租终日睡，得钱沽酒一春狂。
新营茅舍轩窗静，旋煮山蔬匕箸香。
戏集句成图素壁，本来无事却成忙。

东篱幽深冷僻懒得穿衣裳，书卷纵横乱放还杂有药囊。
无吏前来征税只管终日睡，有钱买酒喝整个春天很狂。
新建的茅草屋舍窗明几净，刚煮的野蔬匙筷尝来真香。
游戏集成的诗句写上白壁，本来没有事情却弄得很忙。

I'm too lazy to dress in the east fence deep and lonely,

Where scattered books are mixed with bags of medicine.

No official comes to collect taxes, I just sleep all day,

Having money to buy wine I am crazy all spring.

The windows of newly built hut are clean and bright,

With chopsticks, taste delicious the wild vegetables cooked freshly.

Game like integrated verses are written on the white wall,

I have nothing to do but very busy.

小饮

A Small Drink

莫笑放翁颠，歌呼覆酒船。

双螯初斫雪，珍鲞已披绵。

寒雨连旬日，新橙又一年。

更须重九到，作意菊花前。

不要笑放翁我疯疯颠颠，又唱又喊要把酒船弄翻。

蟹的双螯肉刚刚白如雪，珍贵的鱼鲞已肥厚如绵。

寒冷的雨连着下了十天，新橙上市又将卖上一年。

更是要等重阳佳节到来，才有灵感作诗在菊花前。

Don't laugh at me, Fangweng, to be crazy,

Singing and shouting, I capsized the boat nearly.

The meat of crab's claws is just as white as snow,

The precious fish carp is as thick as cotton already.

The cold rain has been falling for ten days continuously,

For another year the new orange will be on sale.

Wait until the Double Ninth Festival' s arrival,

Before chrysanthemums I have inspiration to write poetry.

新凉

New Cool

菰首初离水，姜芽浅渍糟。
粳香等炊玉，韭美胜炮羔。
露下残芜湿，风生万木号。
从今更何事？痛饮读《离骚》。

香菰的头初步脱水，生姜的芽刚刚腌糟。
粳米饭香如煮白玉，韭菜味美胜烤羊羔。
下露了残草被打湿，风起时万木在呼号。
从今以后还有何事？只有痛饮读读《离骚》。

The mushroom head is dehydrated preliminarily,
The ginger buds have been pickled only.
Like white jade is fragrant japonica rice,
Than roasted lamb, chives taste better.
The grass is wet with dew falling,
When the wind blows, thousands of trees are crying.
What else can I do from now on ?
Only drinking and reading *Lisao* .

夜闻埭东卖酒鼓声哗甚

Hearing Night Noisy Drumming of Liquor at East of the Dam

乌桕森疏照溪赤，
寒鸦翩翻蔽天黑。
鲜鲈出网重兼斤，
新蟹登盘大盈尺。
年年此际清霜夜，
饭罢读书声满舍。
岂惟父子讲家学，
亦有朋侪结经社。
谁令屠沽聚里中，
鼓声终夜聒老翁？
呜呼安得寐无聪，
不但杜老左耳聋？

乌桕树或密或疏把溪水照赤，
寒鸦轻快地翻飞把天空遮黑。
新鲜的鲈鱼出网时有二斤重，
装入盘中的新螃蟹大满一尺。
年年这时候下着清霜的夜晚，
吃罢饭后读书之声充满房舍。
这哪里只是我们父子讲家学，
也有朋友们为学经书而结社。
谁叫屠夫酒商都聚在邻里中，
鼓声响了一夜吵闹我这老翁。
啊呀，我怎能听不见睡得着，
不只是像杜老那样左边耳聋。

Thick or sparse tallow trees turn the stream red,

The sky is darkened by the jackdaws flying up and down.

A fresh bass weighs two jin when it comes out the net,

The new crab in the plate is a foot long.

At this time every year, the sky is frosting,

After dinner, the house is filled with sound of reading.

This is not just our father and son talking about family learning,

There are also friends who have formed groups to learn scriptures.

Who makes butchers and liquor sellers gather in the neighborhood,

The drums ringing all night, making a noise for me, an old man ?

Ah, how can I not hear and get a good sleep ,

Not just left ear is deaf like Mr. Du Fu.

东村

East Village

塘路东头乌柏树，偶携藤杖得幽寻。
桃源阡陌自来往，辋口云山无古今。
远浦过帆供极目，暮天横雁入微吟。
归来更觉愁无那，剩放灯前酒碗深。

塘边路东头都是乌柏树，我偶尔携藤杖去把幽寻。
沿桃源般小路独自来往，退隐地的云山无论古今。
极目可见远处水上过帆，傍晚横飞的雁激发诗情。
归来后更觉得忧愁无奈，只能灯前放一酒碗很深。

The east end of the pond road is covered with tallow trees,
Occasionally, I carry a cane to search for quiet natural scenery.
Walking alone along the path like a paradise,
The clouds and mountains in the retreat don't matter in whether ancient times or today.
From afar, sailing boats can be seen passing in the distant water,
The wild geese flying across the sky in the evening inspire poetic sentiment.
I feel more sad and helpless when I come back,
I can put a deep bowl of wine in front of the lamp only.

九月三日泛舟湖中作

Boating in the Lake on September 3rd

儿童随笑放翁狂，又向湖边上野航。
鱼市人家满斜日，菊花天气近新霜。
重重红树秋山晚，猎猎青帘社酒香。
邻曲莫辞同一醉，十年客里过重阳。

儿童随着放翁嬉笑发狂，又向鉴湖边上去赴野航。
斜阳满满照着鱼市人家，菊花盛开天气近有新霜。
重重红树傍着将晚秋山，青帘猎猎作响社酒飘香。
邻居莫推辞与我同一醉，我曾十年离开家过重阳。

The children laughed and frolicked with me,Fangweng,
And then set sail for the wild by the lake.
The setting sun was shining all over the fish market,
With the new frost near, chrysanthemums were fully blooming.
Layers of red trees stood by the late autumn mountains,
The green curtains were rustling and the wine was the fragrant.
My neighbors didn't refuse to get drunk with me,
I have been away from home for ten years to celebrate the Double Ninth Festival.

归云门

Returning to Yunmen Mountain

万里归来值岁丰，
解装乡墅乐无穷。
甑炊饱雨湖菱紫，
篾络迎霜野柿红。
坏壁尘埃寻醉墨，
孤灯饼饵对邻翁。
微官行矣闽山去，
又寄千岩梦想中。

万里归来正好遇到年丰，
在老屋解行装其乐无穷。
炊甑把经雨的湖菱煮紫，
篾篓装的野柿经霜变红。
拂去坏壁尘埃寻找醉墨，
孤灯下吃糕饼面对邻翁。
我要走了去福建做小官，
又把梦想寄千岩万壑中。

I came back from thousands of miles away just in a bumper year,

Unlocking the luggage in my old house is very happy.

The rainy water caltrops cooked by steamer turn purple,

The frosted wild persimmons in the bamboo basket turn fiery.

Wipe away the dust on the broken wall to search for drunk calligraphies,

Eating cakes under a solitary lamp and facing a neighboring old man.

I'm leaving to serve as a petty official in Fujian,

And place my dreams in innumerable mountains and valleys.

兰亭
Lanting

兰亭绝境擅吾州，病起身闲得纵游。
曲水流觞千古胜，小山丛桂一年秋。
酒酣起舞风前袖，兴尽回桡月下舟。
江左诸贤嗟未远，感今怀昔使人愁。

兰亭是我们地区的绝佳胜境，我病后身稍闲得以纵情畅游。

曲水流觞是千古以来的胜事，小山桂树丛生又是一年之秋。

我酒酣兴起在风前挥袖起舞，兴尽回到月下双桨划动归舟。

可叹啊，江东诸贤尚未走远，感慨今天怀念往昔真使人愁。

Lanting is definitely the best scenic spot in our prefecture,

Leisure after illness, I can indulge in pleasure.

The floating wine cups along winding water has been a fine game since ancient times.

The hill covered with osmanthus trees is another sign of autumn in the year.

I rise and wave my sleeves to dance in wind while drunk,

I return under the moon and paddle my boat home in spirits low.

Alas, the Jiangdong sages have not gone far yet,

Sighing about today and missing the past gives me sorrow.

临安春雨初霁

Just Clear after Spring Rain in Linan

世味年来薄似纱，
谁令骑马客京华？
小楼一夜听春雨，
深巷明朝卖杏花。
矮纸斜行闲作草，
晴窗细乳戏分茶。
素衣莫起风尘叹，
犹及清明可到家。

近年来世间人情味浇薄如纱，
又是谁叫我骑马作客于京华。
小楼上只听得春雨下了一夜，
第二天深巷里有人叫卖杏花。
闲来铺开小纸按斜行作草书，
晴明窗前撇开细沫品味新茶。
不要再感叹风尘将素衣染黑，
我还来得及于清明节赶到家。

The human touch in the world has become as thin as voile in recent years,

Who invites me to ride a horse to visit the capital ?

I listen to the spring rain all night in a small building,

The next day in a deep lane apricot flowers are heard to sell.

At leisure I spread out a piece of paper and scribble in cursive,

In front of a bright window putting aside foams I taste the new tea.

Don't sigh that dust has dyed my white clothes to black,

I still have time to get home before the Qingming Festival.

秋思

Thinking in Autumn

利欲驱人万火牛，江湖浪迹一沙鸥。
日长似岁闲方觉，事大如天醉亦休。
砧杵敲残深巷月，井梧摇落故园秋。
欲舒老眼无高处，安得元龙百尺楼。

利欲驱使着人像万条火牛，我是浪迹江湖的一只沙鸥。
闲时才觉得一日长如一年，天大的事喝醉了也就罢休。
砧杵声把深巷中月亮敲残，井边的梧桐摇落故园之秋。
要想极目远眺苦无登高处，怎能像陈元龙登上百尺楼。

Like thousands of fiery bulls, desire drives people,
Wandering around the whole country, I'm just a seagull.
When I have leisure, I feel a day as long as a year,
Just give up when drunk, even a big deal.
The sound of anvil and pestle knocks the moon in a deep lane down,
The Chinese parasol tree by the well shooks down the autumn of my hometown.
I want to look far but don't have a place to climb,
How can I climb a hundred feet tower like Chen Yuanlong ?

秋思
癸卯

小市

Bazaar

春风小市画桥横，
桥北桥南次第行。
绝景惟诗号勍敌，
闲愁赖酒作长城。
楼台到处灵和柳，
帘幙谁家子晋笙？
薄暮归来渔火闹，
放翁自笑欲忘情。

春风里小市画桥横陈，
桥南桥北我依次而行。
只有诗是美景的劲敌，
闲愁依赖酒作为长城。
楼台到处是灵和殿柳，
帘幕后谁人吹子晋笙。
傍晚归来渔火很热闹，
放翁笑自己几欲忘情。

The Bazaar's bridge like a painting lies in the spring breeze,

I walk in turn from south to north of the bridge.

Only poetry is the powerful enemy of beautiful scenery,

Leisurely sorrow relies on wine as the great wall.

Around the tower there are willows of Linghe Temple everywhere,

Behind the curtain who is playing Zijin Sheng there ?

When I come back at dusk,the fishing fire is very lively,

I, Fangweng, laugh at myself to be delirious with joy.

小雨云门溪上

Light Rain on Yunmen Stream

好雨疏疏压暮埃，断云漠漠带春雷。
离黄穿树语断续，翠碧衔鱼飞去来。
生菜入盘随冷饼，朱樱上市伴青梅。
狂吟不是夸强健，老气如山未许摧。

稀疏的好雨压住了尘埃，密布的碎云带来了春雷。
黄鹂穿飞树间断续而语，翠鸟衔着鱼飞去又飞来。
生菜伴着冷饼装入盘中，红樱桃上市伴随着青梅。
疯狂吟诵不是夸耀强健，老来气概如山不容摧毁。

The sparse good rain covers the evening dust,
The dense broken clouds bring the spring thunder.
Orioles flying through trees sing intermittently,
Kingfishers fly back and forth with fish in beaks.
Lettuce is placed with cold cakes on a tray,
Red cherries come into market with green plums.
Crazy chanting is not boasting about strong and healthy,
The spirit in old age which cannot be destroyed is like a mountain.

秋日郊居

Suburb Residence in Autumn

秋日留连野老家，
朱盘鲊脔粲如花。
已炊藟散真珠米，
更点丁坑白雪茶。

又

车荡比邻例馈鱼，
流涎对此四腮鲈。
北窗雨过凉如水，
消得先生一醉无！

秋天里舍不得离开老农家，
红盘里盛放的鱼块美如花。
珍珠米煮的饭松软如花蕾，
还配有产自丁坑的白雪茶。

与车荡邻近照例易获赠鱼，
我大流口水对此四腮之鲈。
北窗雨过后天气清凉如水，
把先生我一身的醉意消除！

In autumn, I can't bear to leave the old farmhouse,
The fish pieces in the red plate are as beautiful as flowers.
As soft as a flower bud is the rice cooked with pearl rice,
There is also white snow tea prodnced in Dingkeng.

Near a pond named Chedang,I receive fish as gifts routinely,
At this four–gilled bass I drool profusely.
It is as cool as water after the rain at the north window,
And gets rid of drunkenness of me completely.

初冬
Early Winter

已罢弹冠欲挂冠，一庵天遣养衰残。
雨荒园菊枝枝瘦，霜染江枫叶叶丹。
羹釜带鳞烹白小，蓬门和蔓系黄团。
夕阳更动闲游兴，十月吴中未苦寒。

弹劾之事已了我欲自行罢官，老天给我一间茅屋以养残年。

雨使小园菊花荒芜枝枝很瘦，霜把江枫树叶染红叶叶如丹。

汤锅用来烹煮带鳞的小白鱼，蓬门上连藤系着黄南瓜团团。

人到晚年我又动起闲游之兴，吴中虽已十月天气尚未苦寒。

My impeachment is over, but I want to resign,
God gave me a hut to spend my residual years.
The rain made each twig of chrysanthemums thin in garden,
The frost has stained the maple leaves red like cinnabar.
The soup pot is used to cook a small white scaly fish,
Yellow pumpkins are tied with vines on the door of wicker.
I am in the mood to wander again in my old age,
In Wuzhong District, it is not yet very cold, although October.

戏咏山阴风物

Jokingly Chanting Scenery in Shanyin

万里秦吴税驾迟，还乡已叹鬓成丝。
城边绿树山阴道，水际朱扉夏禹祠。
项里杨梅盐可彻，湘湖莼菜豉偏宜。
图经草草常堪恨，好事它年采此诗。

到万里外秦吴做官告退太迟，可叹回到家乡两鬓斑白如丝。
城旁的绿树已形成了山阴道，水边的红漆大门属于夏禹祠。
项里产的杨梅用盐可以腌透，与湘湖莼菜搭配豆豉最相宜。
常恨带画的方志图册很潦草，他年若有好事者请采用此诗。

It is too late to quit office in Qin and Wu thousands of miles away,
Alas, back home, my hair has turned white as silk already.
By the city, green trees have formed the Shanyin Way,
Beside the water, the red gate belongs the Temple of Xia Yu.
The bayberries in Xiangli can be marinated with salt thoroughly.
The water shield in Xianghu is best for fermented soybeans.
I often regret that the illustrated local chronicles are careless and hasty,
Adopt this poem please if in the future there is a busybody.

闲居对食书愧

Writing My Heart of Shame Facing Fine Food when Staying at Home Idle

游宦无功坐免归，
谁令盘箸极甘肥？
锦鳞差尾鱼登俎，
绣羽骈头雉触机。
桑落满壶春盎盎，
雨前輚硙雪霏霏。
残年何地酬君赐，
自古羁臣厌蕨薇。

我在外做官无功被免职而归，
谁使我的饭菜极尽甘甜肥美？
砧板上有尾巴分叉的锦鳞鱼，
一对触碰机关被捉的花野鸡。
满壶桑葚酒暖融融春意盎然，
碾细的雨前茶犹如白雪霏霏。
我已残年何处报答君王恩赐，
自古以来罪臣只能吃厌蕨薇。

As an official outside, I returned home after dismissed for no merit,
Who enables me to enjoy the extremely sweet and plump meals ?
On the cutting board are forked–tail fishes with brocaded scales,
And a pair of trapped pheasants with floral feather.
Full pot of mulberry wine, full of spring atmosphere,
The finely ground tea before the rain is like snow falling profusely.
Where can I reward the king's grace since I have been old already ?
Down the ages, guilty officials can eat ferns only.

偶得长鱼巨蟹，命酒小饮，盖久无此举也

Accidental Acquisition of Long Fish and Giant Crab, a Small Drink Served, Not Having Done This in a Long Time

老生日日困盐齑，
异味棕鱼与楮鸡。
敢望槎头分缩项，
况当霜后得团脐。
堪怜妄出缘香饵，
尚想横行向草泥。
东崦夜来梅已动，
一樽芳酝径须携。

老生我天天摆脱不了吃咸菜，
棕榈花与楮树菌便算换口味。
能吃到鳊鱼怎敢分是否缩项，
何况霜后所得螃蟹竟是团脐。
可怜鳊鱼胡乱出来因贪香饵，
你螃蟹竟还想横行向着草泥。
东山夜来梅花消息已有所动，
直须把一壶芬芳的好酒携去。

I can't get rid of eating pickles every day,

Palm flowers and tree fungus are considered a change of pace.

If I can eat bream, how dare I tell whether it is one necked ?

Let alone, the obtained crab after frost is a round navel one actually.

The poor bream goes out recklessly because of craving for bait,

You crab still wants to run towards the grass and mire.

At night in Dongshan, there is news of plum blossoms,

I just need to bring a pot of fragrant wine there.

霜夜

Frosty Night

梅花欲动梦魂狂，
橙子闲搓指爪香。
莫怪草堂清到骨，
一梳残月伴新霜。

又

黄甘磊落围三寸，
赤蟹轮囷可一斤。
更唤东阳曲道士，
与君霜夜策奇勋。

梅花欲开令我梦魂发狂，
闲来搓弄橙子手指也香。
难怪我的草堂清凉到骨，
原来一梳残月伴着新霜。

黄柑硕大体围有三寸，
圆圆的赤蟹重约一斤。
再唤来东阳的曲道士，
我与君霜夜将它扫尽。

The plum blossoms are about to bloom, making my soul in dream crazy,

My fingers smell fragrant for I rub oranges when I'm free.

No wonder my thatched cottage is so cool,

The waning moon is accompanied by new frost originally.

The orange is big, three inches in circumstance,

The round red crap weighs about one jin.

Then filling a pot of Dongyang wine,

With you I will drink it up in this frosty night.

杂咏园中果子

Narrating Fruits of My Garden in Poetry

不酸金橘种初成，
无核枇杷接亦生。
珍产已从幽圃得，
浊醪仍就小槽倾。

又

浆石榴随糕作节，
蜡樱桃与酪同时。
两株偶向池边种，
可喜今年坠折枝。

不酸的金橘试种初步长成，
无核的枇杷经过嫁接也生。
珍贵的出产已从静园获得，
浑浊的酒仍就着小槽外倾。

浆石榴随糕饼送人过节，
蜡樱桃与奶酪同时上市。
这两株偶然向池边栽种，
可喜今年结果压断树枝。

The non–sour kumquats have been planted experimentally,
The seedless loquats can also be grown through grafting.
Precious produce has been obtained from the secluded garden,
Through the small trough still flows out the turbid wine.

Pomegranates with cakes have been sent for the festival,
Wax cherries and cheese are simultaneously available.
Theses two plants were planted accidentally near the pool,
The fruits of this year have crushed the branches, delightful.

村舍杂书

Miscellaneous Notes on Village Houses

五月新面成，六月甘瓜熟。
作曲及良时，火见金始伏。
悬知桑落后，醅面酡如粥。
再拜谢天公，无功叨美禄。

又

东山石上茶，鹰爪初脱鞲。
雪落红丝硙，香动银毫瓯。
爽如闻至言，余味终日留。
不知叶家白，亦复有此不？

五月新面刚磨成，六月甜瓜已成熟。
作曲得赶好时辰，见火金气才藏伏。
料想桑葚落尽后，酒面浮沫浓如粥。
再次拜谢老天爷，无功享受高俸禄。

东山石冈上的茶，像鹰爪刚脱臂衣。
又像茶磨上落雪，香动银制的茶杯。
爽如闻至理名言，余味无穷终日留。
不知叶家白茶叶，与东山茶可比否？

The new flour has just been ground in May,
In June, the melon has matured already.
Making liquor yeast must be in good time,
Seeing fire, gold hides itself certainly.
I expect, after all the mulberries have fallen,
The floating wine foam will be as thick as porridge,
Thank God again,
I have no merit, but enjoy a high salary.

The tea on the stone hill in Dongshan,
Just as eagle claws take off bridle.
Like snow falling on the red tea mill,
From a silver tea cup rises a sweet smell.
As refreshing as hearing a wise saying,
It has an endless aftertaste all day long.
I woder if the white tea from the Ye family can compare with Dongshan tea ?

戏咏乡里食物示邻曲

Jokingly Chanting Rural Food to Neighbors

山阴古称小蓬莱，
青山万叠环楼台。
不惟人物富名胜，
所至地产皆奇瑰。
茗芽落硙压北苑，
药苗入馔逾天台。
明珠百舸载芡实，
火齐千担装杨梅。
湘湖莼长涎正滑，
秦望蕨生拳未开。
箭萌蛰藏待时雨，
桑蕈菌蠢惊春雷。
稷花蒸煮蘸醯酱，
姜茁披剥腌糟醅。
细研罂粟具汤液，
湿裹山蓣供炮煨。
老馋自觉笔力短，
得一忘十真堪咍。
从今置之勿复道，
一瓢陋巷师颜回。

山阴古时候被称作小蓬莱，
青山万重环绕着它的楼台。
不仅人物中多有才俊之士，
所到之处出产都丰富多彩。
刚磨好的芽茶压倒了北苑，
算作食材的药苗超过天台。
百艘船载着明珠样的芡实，
千副担装有宝石似的杨梅。
湘湖莼菜的黏液长而且滑，
秦望山生的野蕨卷曲未开。
竹笋蛰伏躲藏着等待时雨，
桑耳如菌类丛生惊闻春雷。
稷花经过蒸煮可蘸酱醋吃，
姜芽被披剥可腌可糟可醅。
罂粟细细地研碎会有汤液，
湿裹的山芋可在火灰里煨。
老饕我自己觉得笔力不够，
记得一样忘掉十样真堪悲。
从今将此事搁下不再重提，
要学居陋巷一瓢饮的颜回。

In ancient times, Shanyin was called little Penglai.

Its towers are surrounded by layers of mountains green.

Not only are there many talented individuals,

Everywhere we go, our there are abundant and diverse products.

The newly ground bud tea overwhelms Beiyuan,

Exceed Tiantai, the medicinal seedlings counted as ingredients.

Hundreds of boats carry pearl–like gorgon fruits,

Thousands of pairs of baskets contain gem–like waxberries.

The mucus of Xianghu water shield is long and slippery,

The wild ferns of Qinwang Mountain are curly and unopened.

Bamboo shoots are hidden while waiting for timely rain.

The clumps of woody fungus seem to hear the sound of spring thunder.

After steaming, flowers can be dipped in soy sauce and vinegar to eat,

Peeled ginger sprouts can be pickled or fermented to eat.

Fine grinding of poppy will result in soup,

Wet–wrapped yams can be simmered in fire ashes to eat.

I, a glutton, feel my writing ability is not good enough,

Remembering one thing, forgetting ten things, It's a ridicule,

Put this matter aside from now on and never bring it up again.

Learn from Yan Hui, who lived in a humble alley and drank with a ladle.

对酒

Drinking

素月度银汉，红螺斟玉醪。
染丹梨半颊，斫雪蟹双螯。
诗就吟逾苦，杯残兴尚豪。
闲愁剪不断，剩欲借并刀。

皎洁的月亮渡过银河，红螺杯中斟满了美酒。
梨的半边被染成丹红，蟹的双螯有雪白的肉。
诗写成吟起来愈觉苦，酒快喝完了意兴尚豪。
无端的忧愁剪之不断，颇想从并州借来快刀。

The bright and clear moon crosses the Milky Way,
The red snail cup is filled with good wine.
Half of the pear is dyed red like cinnabar,
The crab's claws have snow–white meat.
The more I mite and recite the poem,the more I feel the bitterness,
When wine almost finished, I am still in high spirits.
Unreasonable sorrow can not be cut off,
I want to borrow a sharp knife from Bingzhou really.

又

密筱持苫屋，寒芦用织帘。
彘肩柴熟罨，莼菜豉初添。
黄甲如盘大，红丁似蜜甜。
街头桑叶落，相唤指青帘。

细竹拿来遮盖屋顶，芦苇用以编织门帘。
蹄髈已用柴火焖熟，莼菜中豆豉酱刚添。
黄黄的螃蟹大如盘，红红的蕈羹似蜜甜。
街头的桑叶已飘落，路人相唤指指酒帘。

Fine bamboo is fetched to cover the roof,
Cold reeds are used to weave the door curtain.
The hooves have been braised with firewood,
The water shield has just been added with fermented soybean paste.
The yellow crab is as big as a plate,
The red mushroom soup is as sweet as honey.
The mulberry leaves on the street have all fallen,
Passers call each other, pointing to the wine curtain.

纵笔

Indulging in Writing

百尺松根结茯苓，
千年长养似人形。
谁知金鼎烹初熟，
恰值山翁醉欲醒。

百尺高的松树根上结茯苓，
经过千年成长养成了人形。
谁知用金鼎烹煮刚刚成熟，
恰好碰到山翁酒醉刚要醒。

Poria cocos grows on the root of a hundred–foot pine tree,
After thousands of years it grows into the shape of a man.
Who knows it has just been cooked in a golden cauldron,
Coincidentally about to wake up, the drunk old man.

自适

Self Adjustment

远游思里巷，
久困念耕桑。
家酿倾醇碧，
园蔬摘矮黄。
利名因醉远，
日月为闲长。
今岁虽中熟，
吾徒亦小康。

出门在外常会思念家乡，
穷困久了就想种田栽桑。
倒杯醇香碧绿的家酿酒，
从小园摘来青菜矮脚黄。
名和利因喝醉酒而远离，
岁月因人闲而显得漫长。
今年的收成虽然是中等，
我们的生活也算是小康。

癸卯 國鉀寫

When we are away from home, we often miss our hometown,
We want to farm and plant mulberry if poor long.
We pour a glass of mellow green home–brewed wine,
And pick dwarf yellow vegetables from the garden.
We stay away from fame and gain when drunken,
Time seems very long because we are idle.
Although this year's harvest is moderate,
Our lives will also be faily well–off.

禹祠

Yu Temple

祠宇嵯峨接宝坊，
扁舟又系画桥傍。
豉添满箸莼丝紫，
蜜渍堆盘粉饵香。
团扇卖时春渐晚，
夹衣换后日初长。
故人零落今何在，
空吊颓垣墨数行。

祠堂巍峨连接着石牌坊，

我的小船又系在画桥旁。

添豆豉把满筷莼丝染紫，

盘里堆着蜜渍粉饵很香。

卖团扇的时候春已渐晚，

换上夹衣白昼开始变长。

昔日朋友凋零今在何处，

空自凭吊破墙墨迹数行。

The tall ancestral temple is connected with a stone memorial archway,

My boat is tied to the bridge again.

Adding fermented soybeans makes the full chopsticks of water shield purple,

Candied powder bait piled on the plate is sweet–smelling.

When it comes to selling round fans, spring is getting late,

When people put on their jackets, the days begin to lengthen.

Where are my old friends who have become less and less,

I can't help but visit and ponder ink marked on the broken wall.

初夏行平水道中

On the Way to Pingshui in Early Summer

老去人间乐事稀，一年容易又春归。
市桥压担莼丝滑，村店堆盘豆荚肥。
傍水风林莺语语，满园烟草蝶飞飞。
郊行已觉侵微暑，小立桐阴换夹衣。

人老了在世间快乐事儿变少，一年很容易过去春天又回归。

集市桥上满担莼丝滑腻可口，村店盘里堆的水煮豆荚肥美。

傍水林中随风传来声声莺语，满园碧草如烟蝴蝶来去翻飞。

初夏郊行稍久便觉暑气袭人，我在桐荫站立片刻更换夹衣。

Old age makes me feel the world less happy,

It's easy for a year to pass and spring to come quickly.

On the market bridge, full load of water shields are smooth and delicious,

The poached pods piled up on the village shop plate are tasty.

From the forest by water comes with the wind warblers singing,

In the garden full of misty grass,butterflies are flying back and forth.

During my outing in the suburbs in early summer,I felt the summer heat slightly,

To change my clothes I stood in the shade of sycamore tree shortly.

西村

West Village

乱山深处小桃源，往岁求浆忆叩门。
高柳簇桥初转马，数家临水自成村。
茂林风送幽禽语，坏壁苔侵醉墨痕。
一首清诗记今夕，细云新月耿黄昏。

万山丛中有个小小的桃花源，记得当年讨水喝曾敲人家门。
高柳簇拥的桥上刚勒转马头，就见河边几户人家自然成村。
风吹茂林不见啼鸟但闻鸣声，我曾醉题的残壁已布满苔痕。
忽有一首小诗记下今晚夜景，轻云之中一弯新月烛照黄昏。

Deep in the mountains there is a small Peach Garden,
I remember I knocked on a door to ask for water drinking.
When the horse turned its head on the willow clustered bridge,
I saw several houses by the river naturally forming a village.
The wind blew the songs of unseen birds through the forest lush,
The ink marks I wrote on the remnant wall while drunk have been covered by moss.
Suddenly, a fresh poem occurs to me to record the scene of tonight,
With a crescent moon among the light clouds illuminating the dusk.

幽居初夏

My Quiet House in Early Summer

湖山胜处放翁家，
槐柳阴中野径斜。
水满有时观下鹭，
草深无处不鸣蛙。
箨龙已过头番笋，
木笔犹开第一花。
叹息老来交旧尽，
睡来谁共午瓯茶。

湖光山色最佳处是放翁我的家，
槐和柳的树阴中有条野径横斜。
湖水满溢时我常观看白鹭下翔，
草木幽深处到处是鸣叫的青蛙。
箨龙竹笋已经被人挖过头一番，
笔一样的辛夷花还开着第一茬。
我感叹老来亲朋好友纷纷离世，
午睡醒来谁能与我共饮一壶茶。

My home is the best place for enjoying the scenery of the lakes and hills,
A wild path slants in the shade of locust and willow trees.
I often watch egrets flying down when the lake overspills,
The frogs are croaking everywhere deep in the grasses.
The first batch of bamboo shoots have been dug already,
For the first time, the pen like magnolia flower is still blooming,
Alas, many of my old friends have passed away in old age,
Who can share a pot of tea with me after waking up from siesta.

游山西村

Visiting the Village West of the Mountain

莫笑农家腊酒浑，丰年留客足鸡豚。
山重水复疑无路，柳暗花明又一村。
箫鼓追随春社近，衣冠简朴古风存。
从今若许闲乘月，拄杖无时夜叩门。

莫笑农家腊月酿的酒浑，丰年鸡猪足够招待客人。

山重水复疑无道路可走，柳暗花明过后又是一村。

春社临近村民吹箫打鼓，衣帽简朴古风依旧保存。

今后若许踏月悠闲前来，我会拄杖随时夜来敲门。

Don't laugh at the turbid wine brewed by farmers in the twelfth lunar month,
Chickens and pigs are enough to entertain guests in a good year.
After crossing layers of mountains and rivers I doubt there is no way,
But behind the clustering willows comes another village with flowers gay.
When the Spring Sacrifice Day draws near, villagers play the flute and drum,
Wearing simple clothes and hats, they still keep ancient customs.
From now on, if allowed to come leisurely while the moon is bright,
I'll come with a cane to knock on the door at any time at night.

沈园

The Shen Garden

城上斜阳画角哀，
沈园非复旧池台。
伤心桥下春波绿，
曾是惊鸿照影来。

又

梦断香消四十年，
沈园柳老不吹绵。
此身行作稽山土，
犹吊遗踪一泫然。

城头挂着斜阳，画角之声悲哀，
沈园不再是往日的小池楼台。
伤心桥下流淌着碧绿的春水，
曾有美人以水为镜照其丰采。

自她离世我已梦断四十年，
沈园的柳树老了不再吹绵。
我这身体快要成稽山之土，
还要凭吊遗踪，泪下潸然。

The setting sun hangs over the city, and the sound of horn is mournful,
The Shen Garden is no longer the small pavilions and ponds of the past.
Under the heart-broken bridge flows a green spring river,
There used to be a beauty who looked in its water as a mirror.

It has been 40 years since my dream broke as she had passed away,
The old willows' catkins in the Shen Garden don't fly any way.
My body is about to be buried under the Kuaiji Mountain and become dust,
I still need visit the traces and have tears trickling down my cheeks.

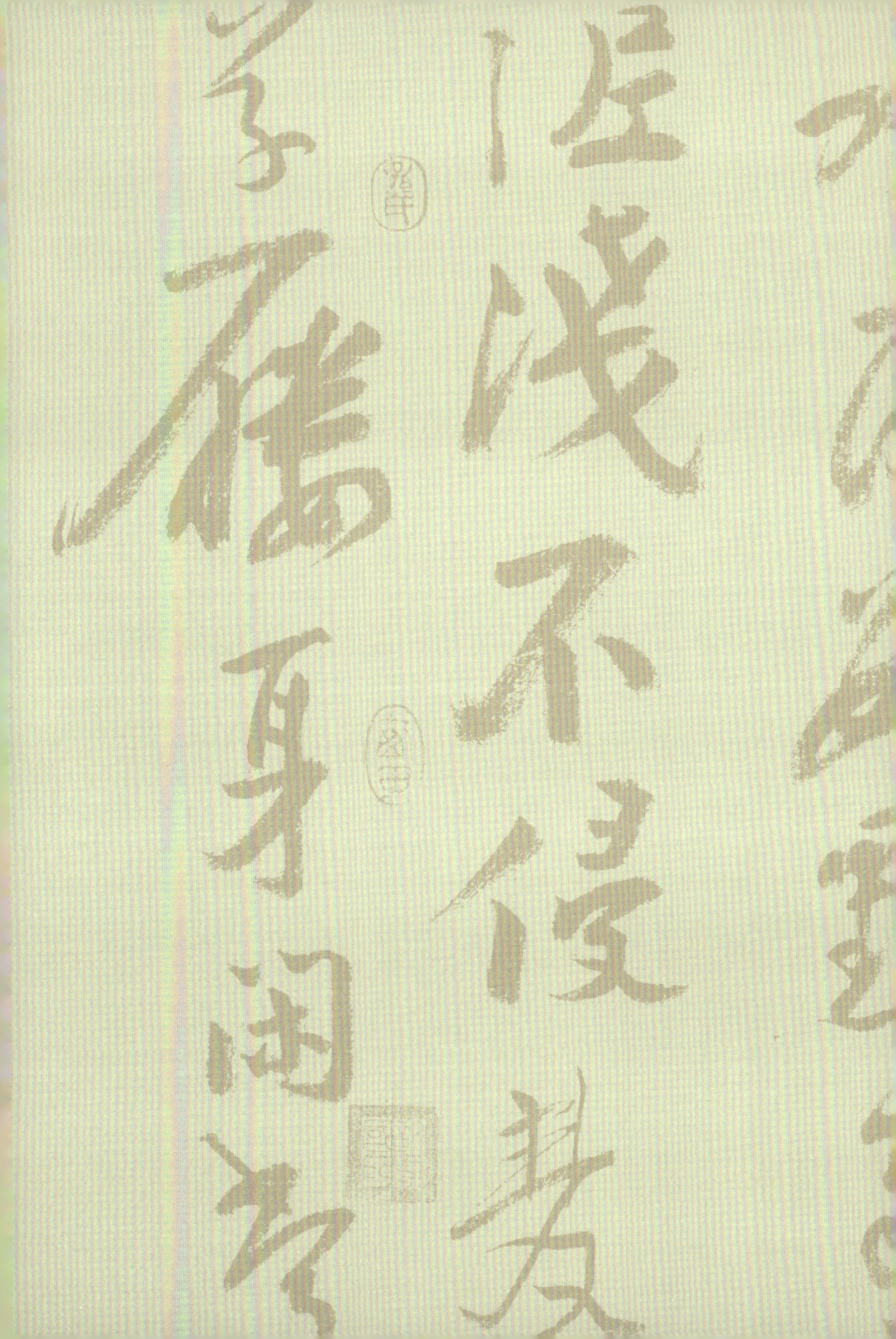

陆游

词 

Poetry

恋绣衾

Loving Embroidered Quilt

不惜貂裘换钓篷,嗟时人、谁识放翁?
归棹借樵风稳,数声闻、林外暮钟。

幽栖莫笑蜗庐小,有云山、烟水万重。
半世向丹青看,喜如今、身在画中。

我不惜以名贵的貂裘换钓鱼的船篷,可叹当代人有谁懂我放翁?
归舟借着樵风行得很稳,只听得山林外响起数声暮钟。

不要笑我幽居的草庐狭小,我有如云之山和似烟之水万重。
这些美景我前半生只在图画里看,如今令人欣喜的是身在画中。

I don't hesitate to trade my precious mink fur for a fishing boat canopy,

Alas, who in the world understands me,Fangweng ?

With the woodcutter wind, my returning boat is sailing steadily,

I can hear outside the mountain forest several twilight bells ringing vaguely.

Don't laugh at the small hut where I live in seclusion,

I have layers of mountains cloudy and water misty.

For the first half of my life I see these sceneries in pictures only,

What's delightful now is that I have been in the picture already.

一竿風月一蓑煙雨家在釣臺西住賣魚生怕近城門況肯到紅塵深處
潮生理棹潮平系纜潮落浩歌歸去時人錯把比嚴光我自是無名漁夫
癸卯初冬寫放翁鵲橋僊詞意

鹊桥仙

Fairy on Magpie Bridge

一竿风月，一蓑烟雨，家在钓台西住。
卖鱼生怕近城门，况肯到红尘深处？

潮生理棹，潮平系缆，潮落浩歌归去。
时人错把比严光，我自是无名渔父。

垂一钓竿于风月中，披一蓑衣在烟雨里，我家在钓台西边住。
卖鱼生怕靠近城门，何况去俗世深处？

潮涨时划桨行船，潮平时系好船缆，潮落时高歌归去。
人们误把我比作严光，而我实是无名的渔夫。

In wind and moon I hold a pole angling,
Wearing a straw cape against the misty rain.
My home is in the west of the fishing platform.
I fear approaching the city gate on fish selling,
Let alone go deep into the secular world.

On rising tide, I go paddling,

On slack tide, I have my boat moored with a chain.

On falling tide, I sing aloud to return.

People wrongly compare me to the hermit Yan Guang,

However, I am just an unknown old fisherman.

鹧鸪天

Partridges in the Sky

懒向青门学种瓜，只将渔钓送年华。
双双新燕飞春岸，片片轻鸥落晚沙。

歌缥缈，舻呕哑，酒如清露鲊如花。
逢人问道归何处，笑指船儿此是家。

懒得前往京城的青门学种瓜,我只希望打鱼垂钓送走年华。
一双双新燕飞掠春天的河岸,一片片轻鸥落在傍晚的平沙。

歌声隐约传来,船儿声音嘈杂,酒如清露,鱼鲊如花。
每当有人问我归向哪里,我笑指船说:这是我家。

I don't want to learn how to grow melons in Qingmen,
Only wishing to pass my time by angling and fishing.
Pairs of new swallows tly over the riverbanks in spring,
Sheets of light gulls land on the sand in the evening.

Songs sound faint, boats are noisy.
Wine is like clear dew, pickled fish tastes dainty.
Whenever being asked where I'm going finally,
Pointing to the boat, "This is my home!" I say smilingly.

驛外斷橋邊寂寞開無主已是黃昏獨自愁更著風和雨無意苦爭春一任羣芳妒零落成泥碾

卜算子 · 咏梅

Song of Divination:Ode to the Plum Blossom

驿外断桥边,寂寞开无主。
已是黄昏独自愁,更着风和雨。

无意苦争春,一任群芳妒。
零落成泥碾作尘,只有香如故。

驿站外面的断桥旁边,它寂寞地开花,无人关注。
已是黄昏,它独自忧愁,再加上刮风下雨。

它无意争妍斗艳,任凭百花忌妒。
即使凋零落地被碾压成土,也只会留下清香如故。

By the broken bridge outside the post station,

The plum blossom blooms lonely, no one pays it attention.

At dusk already, it feels sad alone,

With wind and rain in addition.

Despite other flowers' envy,

It has no desire to struggle for spring.

Even falling and being crushed into dust,

It only leaves its former fragrance in continuation.

点绛唇

Rouged Lips

采药归来，独寻茅店沽新酿。
暮烟千嶂，处处闻渔唱。

醉弄扁舟，不怕黏天浪。
江湖上，遮回疏放。作个闲人样。

我采药归来，独自找家村店买新酿的酒喝。
傍晚烟霭笼罩的千座山峰，处处听得见渔歌唱和。

醉后摆弄小舟，不怕接天的浪头。
这一回，我在江湖上无拘无束。做个闲散之人四处云游。

Returning from picking herbs,
I alone found a thatched inn to buy newly brewed wine.
In the evening, thousands of peaks are covered by mist,
And filled with the sound of fishing songs.

When drunk, I went boating,
Not fearing waves like a mountain.
This time, I'm unconstraint in rivers and lakes. wanton,
I will be an idler, everywhere roaming.

鹊桥仙

Fairy of the Magpie Bridge

华灯纵博,雕鞍驰射,谁记当年豪举?
酒徒一半取封侯,独去作江边渔父。

轻舟八尺,低篷三扇,占断蘋洲烟雨。
镜湖元自属闲人,又何必官家赐与!

在华灯下纵情赌博,骑着雕鞍马奔驰射猎,可如今谁还记得当年那些壮举?
那些终日酣饮的酒徒大都封了侯,只有我独自去江边打鱼。

我的小船,低篷三扇,长八尺,却尽享烟水迷离之致。
镜湖原来就属于闲人,又何必要君王恩赐!

Under glorious lights, indulging in gambling,
On a carve-saddled horse galloping and shooting,
Who remembers those of my heroic undertaking ?
Half of the drinkers are conferred dukedoms,
Only I go to the riverside fishing.

My small boat is eight-foot long, with three low-hanging sails,
With it I can enjoy great sight of vast misty river.
The Mirror Lake originally belongs to idlers,
Why should I ask the emperor's favor ?

乌夜啼

Crows Crying at Night

纨扇婵娟素月，纱巾缥缈轻烟。
高槐叶长阴初合，清润雨余天。

弄笔斜行小草，钩帘浅醉闲眠。
更无一点尘埃到，枕上听新蝉。

纨制的团扇美如皓月，纱作的头巾似雾如烟。
高槐叶长刚刚成阴，雨后仍是清凉润湿天。

我写字常作斜行草书，小醉后钩起帘儿闲眠。
家里没有一点尘埃，我枕着枕头听新蝉。

The round fan is beautiful like the moon bright,

The gauze kerchief looks faint like smoke light.

The high locust tree has long leaves just to make a shade,

The weather still remains moist and cool after the rain.

I often write in cursive script irregularly,

Rolling up curtains after drinking I sleep leisurely.

My house is very clean without any dust,

Upon my pillow I hear new cicadas chirping happily.

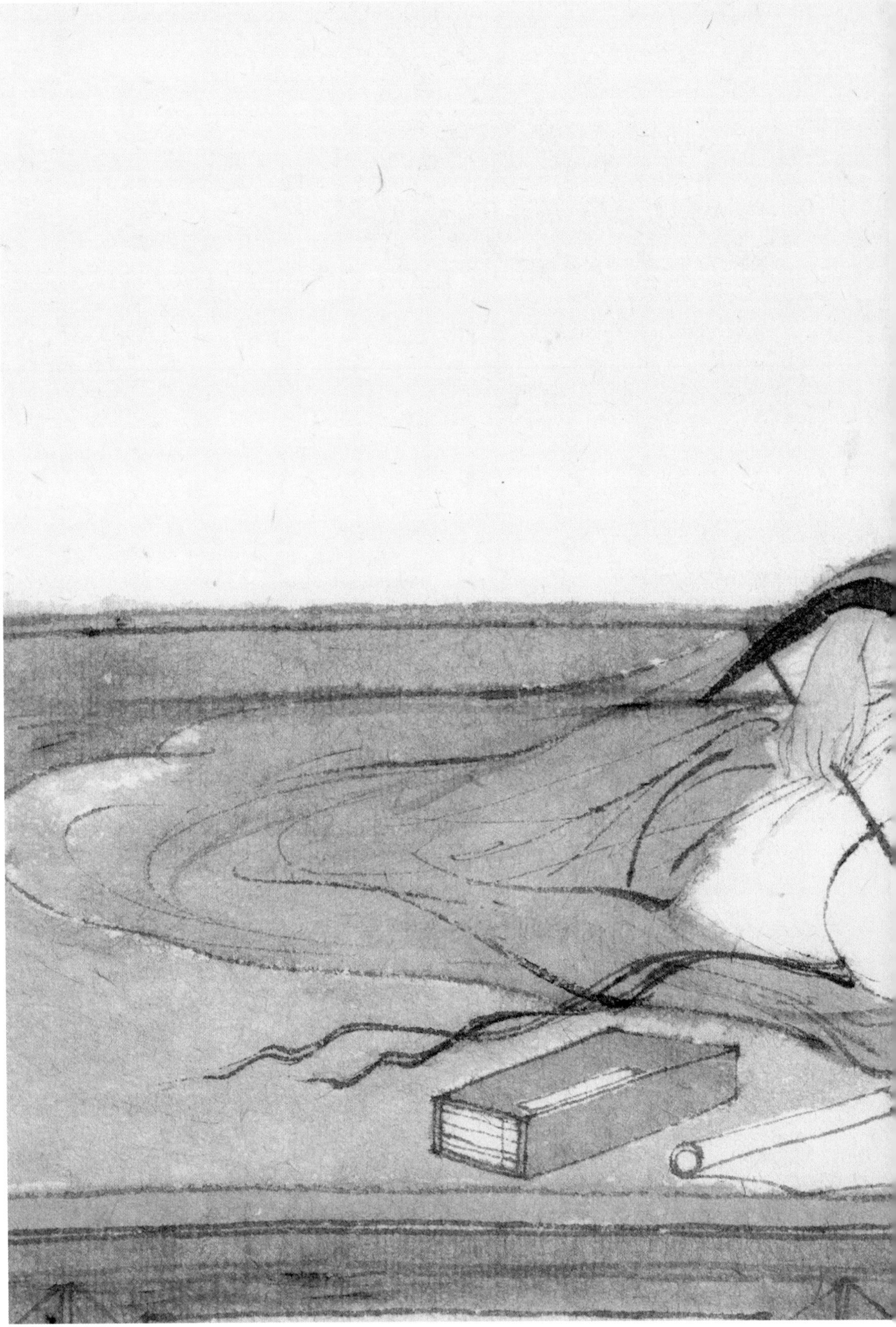

渔歌子

A Fisherman's Song

镜湖俯仰两青天，
万顷玻璃一叶船。
拈棹舞，拥蓑眠，
不作天仙作水仙。

镜湖清澈俯仰两望都是青天，
一叶小舟行在万顷玻璃上面。
挥着桨而舞，抱着蓑衣在眠，
我不愿做天仙而要做个水仙。

Looking up or down, the Mirror Lake is all blue.
As on a vast expanse of glass a small boat is sailing.
Dancing with oars and sleeping in a coir raincoat,
I don't want to be a celestial being but a water being.

长相思

Everlasting Longing for Each Other

暮山青，暮霞明。
梦笔桥头艇子横。
蘋风吹酒醒。

看潮生，看潮平，
小住西陵莫较程。
莼丝初可烹。

傍晚的山青，傍晚的霞明。
梦笔桥头横停着小艇。
微风将醉酒人吹醒。

看着潮生，看着潮平，
在西陵渡小住莫要计较行程。
莼菜刚好可以烹饪。

The mountain is green in the evening, the rosy clouds glow in the evening,

At the end of Mengbi Bridge a small boat is parking.

The gentle breeze woke up the drunken man.

Watch the tide rising, watch the tide leveling,

Don’t worry about the journey when staying for a few days in Xiling Ferry.

The water shield is just for cooking.

陸放翁鷓鴣天詞意
癸卯國鉊寫

鹧鸪天

Partridges in the Sky

家住苍烟落照间，丝毫尘事不相关。
斟残玉瀣行穿竹，卷罢《黄庭》卧看山。

贪啸傲，任衰残，不妨随处一开颜。
元知造物心肠别，老却英雄似等闲！

我的家青烟缭绕夕阳灿烂，人间之事与我毫不相关。
喝完玉瀣酒，穿行竹林间，卷起道家《黄庭经》，躺着看看山。

我贪图歌咏自得，任凭身体衰残，何妨每到一处快快乐乐笑开颜。
我本知道造物主与常人心肠不一般，英雄白白地老去，他却视作等闲！

My home is filled with blue mist and the sunset is brilliant,
Not caring anything about the world of human being.
I walked through the bamboo forest after drinking Yuxie wine,
Rolling up the *Scripture of the Yellow Court*, I lie down to look at the mountains.

I enjoy myself in singing and let my body weaken,
Why not go everywhere and smile happily ?
I know the creator's heart is very particular,
He treats it as unimportant that a hero grows old in vain.

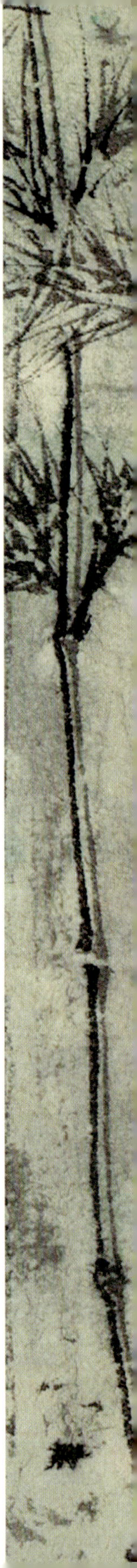

后记

编写一本有意思的书献给陆游诞辰900周年，是绍兴文旅人一直想做的一件事。而此书的呈现则缘起于周向勤老先生给绍兴市市长的一封信。

周向勤是扬州大学外语学院的退休教授，长期从事中英诗文互译和比较文学研究，对陆游的诗文情有独钟，曾想出版《汉英文白对照陆游诗词选》，但因故未能列入出版社的出版计划，于是在2022年底的某一天，给绍兴市市长施惠芳写了封信，施市长非常重视文化人的诉求，批示让我们研究。在具体办理过程中，我们不断地与周教授交流、沟通和磨合，并听取包括出版社、高校、陆游学术研究团体的意见，并结合想编一本有意思的书代表家乡献给陆游诞辰900周年这一初心，最终确定了这本以陆游咏越诗(词)为主，中英文白对照，图文并茂的书。由周向勤先生和绍兴市文史研究馆副馆长李永鑫先生共同在众多陆游乡情诗(词)中精选出60首代表作，并各自作白话释读；周向勤先生对60首诗(词)作英语翻译；浙江画院专职画师吕国钢先生依据每首诗意，原创60幅精美中国画作品作为补充。整部书的编辑、创作、出版历时一年半，其间得到了绍兴文理学院、绍兴市文史研究馆和相关陆游研究机构、专家、学者的关注和支持。

绍兴是历史文化名城、东亚文化之都，越中山水养育了无数名人志士，千古风流、旷世诗魂，而陆游是其中重要的代表。纵观陆游"六十年间万首诗"所构建的多彩而壮阔的境界，无论是慷慨激越的爱国诗，而是清丽隽永的山水诗，其实质都体现于对家乡的热爱、对国家的忠诚。读这本咏越乡情诗，我们可以读出：陆游以天下为已任的博大胸襟重新审视山水之根，从而赋予稽山鉴水以高远的审美感受和深邃的哲理体验。

文学作品中的一切自然景物，都是作者心境的表露，即"人化的自然"，带有作者主观情感，因此，题材本身不能决定诗人的风格。而陆游则有意识地选取足以表现自己艺术风格的自然景物入诗，以物态来表现心态。陆游的山水诗，既表现了山水的清新秀明，反映了对人生的达观与悟境，也传达出了他求真向善的内心世界。特别是陆游写故乡绍兴的诗，这里的山水风光正是江南形胜，“村村皆画本，处处有诗材”，这使他的山水诗有较好的描摹蓝本，相辅相成，相得益彰，成为中国古代山水诗的极致。这也正是我们编写这样一本书，让更多的外国朋友了解绍兴、读懂江南的目的。

在新书即将付梓之际，作为该书的策划者和主编，写此后记，感谢施惠芳市长、周向勤教授、吕国钢老师、李永鑫老师以及我的同事们、众多为此书提供过帮助指导的专家、学者们。

何俊杰　癸卯年三月初二于古城仓桥

（绍兴市文史研究馆副馆长，

时任市委宣传部副部长、市文广旅游局局长）

Epilogue

To compose an interesting book dedicated to the 900th anniversary of Lu You's birth is an idea that practitioners of Shaoxing Culture and Tourism have always wanted to do. And the presentation of this book originated from a letter Mr. Zhou Xiangqin sent to the Mayor of Shaoxing City.

Mr. Zhou, a retired professor of Yangzhou University School of Foreign Languages, has long been engaged in the study of Chinese and English poetry translation and comparative literature, and has a special interest for the poems and literature of Lu You (1125 - 1210), a Chinese historian and poet of the Southern

Song Dynasty. Prof. Zhou once planned to publish a book entitled "Selected Poems and Lyrics by Lu You (Chinese−English version)". However, due to some reasons, the book was not included in the publishing house's schedules. So, one day at the end of 2022, he wrote a letter to Mr. Shi Huifang, the Mayor of Shaoxing City. Mayor Shi has always attached great importance to the demands of cultural people and instructed us to study it. During the specific process of handling the matter, we constantly exchanged, communicated and coordinated with Prof. Zhou, listened to the opinions from publishing houses, universities, and Lu You academic research groups, and combined with our original aspiration of compiling an interesting book to dedicate to the 900th anniversary of Lu You ' s birth, we finally decided to present this book based on Lu You's rhyme poems (shi) and lyrics (ci) with colorful illustrations in Chinese−English languages. Sixty representative works from many poems and lyrics about Lu You's hometown in this book were selected jointly by Prof. Zhou Xiangqin and Mr. Li Yongxin the deputy director of Shaoxing Museum of Literature and History, and interpreted them in vernacular Chinese. Prof. Zhou translated all the 60 poems and lyrics from Chinese into English. Mr. Lv Guogang, a full−time painter of Zhejiang Painting Academy, created 60 original exquisite Chinese paintings based on the meaning of each poem and lyrics. The editing, creation and publication of the whole book took one and a half years. During the time, it received attention and support from Shaoxing

University of Arts and Sciences, Shaoxing Museum of Literature and History, and other relevant research institutions, experts and scholars on Lu You.

Shaoxing is a well-known historic and cultural city, as well as the cultural capital of East Asia. The mountains and rivers of Yuezhong have nurtured countless famous figures and scholars, with timeless charm and unparalleled poetic spirit. Among them, Lu You is a critical representative. Throughout the colorful and magnificent realm constructed by Lu You's "Sixty Years of Ten Thousand Poems and Lyrics", whether it is a passionate patriotic or a beautiful and meaningful landscape poem, its essence is reflected in his love for the hometown and his loyalty to the country. Reading this book, we could touch the heart of Lu You, re-examined the roots of mountains and rivers with his broad mind of taking the world as his responsibility, thus endowing Kuaiji Mountain and Jianhu Lake with a lofty aesthetic feeling and profound philosophical experience.

Natural scenes in literary works are expressions of the author's mood, that is, "humanized nature", with the author's subjective emotions. Therefore, the subject matter itself cannot determine the poet's style. However, Lu You consciously selected natural scenes that could express his artistic style into his poems, and used the physical state to express his state of mind. Lu You's landscape poems and lyrics not only exhibited the freshness and beauty of mountains and rivers, but also reflected his optimism and enlightenment of life, and convey his inner world of seeking truth and goodness. In particular, the poems written by Lu You in Shaoxing, his hometown, where the landscape was the best in the south of the Yangtze River. "Every village is a painting book, and there are poetic materials everywhere", which made his landscape poems had a better blueprint for description, complementary and mutually beneficial, becaming the ultimate of ancient Chinese landscape poetry. This is precisely the goal of our compiling such a book to let more foreign friends understand Shaoxing and Jiangnan. This is precisely the purpose of writing such a book to help more foreign friends understand Shaoxing and areas south of the Yangtze River, China.

The book is about to be published, as the planner and editor–in–chief, I would like to express my deep appreciates to Mayor Shi Huifang, Professor Zhou Xiangqin, Mr. Lv Guogang, Mr. Li Yongxin, as well as my colleagues and many experts and scholars who provided helpful support and guidance for the book.

He Junjie

Deputy Director of Shaoxing Museum of Literature and History/Former Deputy Director of the Municipal Propaganda Department/Former Director of the Municipal Bureau of Culture, Broadcasting, Television and Tourism

Ancient city Cangqiao, the second day of the third month of the Guimao year

图书在版编目（CIP）数据

放翁乡韵：陆游咏越诗词选编 / 绍兴市文化广电旅游局编. -- 杭州：西泠印社出版社，2024.5. -- ISBN 978-7-5508-4508-4

Ⅰ. I222

中国国家版本馆 CIP 数据核字第 2024QX6945 号

放翁乡韵：陆游咏越诗词选编

绍兴市文化广电旅游局　编

责任编辑　傅笛扬
责任出版　冯斌强
责任校对　徐　岫
装帧设计　浙江越生文化创意有限公司
出版发行　西泠印社出版社
（杭州市西湖文化广场32号5楼　邮政编码：310014）
电　　话　0571-87240395
经　　销　全国新华书店
印　　刷　绍兴市越生彩印有限公司
开　　本　787mm×1092mm　1/16
字　　数　125千字
印　　张　14.25
书　　号　ISBN 978-7-5508-4508-4
版　　次　2024年5月第1版　第1次印刷
定　　价　198.00元

西泠印社出版社发行部联系方式：（0571）87243079